I0734507

# MARY CRAWFORD

# THE *Long Road* TO *Love*

## A HIDDEN HEARTS NOVELLA 2

# COPYRIGHT

Published on November 6, 2018, by Diversity Ink Press and Mary Crawford. Author may be reached at MaryCrawfordAuthor.com.

Republish date: August 1, 2019.

Originally published as The Christmas Message

ISBN: 978-1-945637-50-6

Cover by Covers Unbound.

# HIDDEN BEAUTY SERIES

Until the Stars Fall from the Sky

So the Heart Can Dance

Joy and Tiers

Love Naturally

Love Seasoned

Love Claimed

If You Knew Me (and other silent musings)
(novella)

Jude's Song

The Price of Freedom (novella)

Paths Not Taken

Dreams Change (novella)

Heart Wish (100% charity release)

Tempting Fate

The Letter

The Power of Will

# HIDDEN HEARTS SERIES

Identity of the Heart

Sheltered Hearts

Hearts of Jade

Port in the Storm (novella)

Love is More Than Skin Deep

Tough

Rectify

Pieces (a crossover novel)

Hearts Set Free

Freedom (a crossover novel)

The Long Road to Love (novella)

Love and Injustice (Protection Unit)

Out of Thin Air (Protection Unit)

Soul Scars (Protection Unit)


OTHER WORKS:

The Power of Dictation

Vision of the Heart

#AmWriting: A Collection of Letters to Benefit The
Wayne Foundation

# DEDICATION

To those who have been
led to believe they are somehow
worthless and unlovable.

May you find the strength to
love yourself in spite of your flaws
— or perhaps because of them.

And if you're one of the lucky ones,
you'll find someone else to love you
as you should have been loved
all along.

# CHAPTER ONE

# NANCY

My heart breaks as I glance around Paint Your Art Out. I don't even recognize it as the quaint little arts and crafts store I left behind a couple weeks ago before I went into the hospital. It looks more like a disaster area. My once neat display shelves are in complete disarray and inventory is strewn everywhere. Some valuable pieces lay shattered on the ground. My window displays look like someone stomped on them. Looking closer, I smell the distinct odor of vomit. Befuddled, I turn to Libby Mayfield for answers, "What happened here?"

Trying to disguise her nerves, Libby shrugs as she averts her gaze. "I guess one of the temp people Stephanie hired to cover for the holidays decided to hold her bachelorette party here and things got a little wild."

I raise an eyebrow. "Obviously. Why didn't this employee help clean up the mess she created?" I ask as bone rattling fatigue sets in.

"Stephanie took her keys and banned her from the facility."

All my carefully reserved strength flows out of my body as I concede, "Come to think of it, that was probably a good idea. I just don't know how I'm going to clean up this whole mess."

"I'm sorry, Mrs. Lyons. I wasn't working because I had exams last week."

"It's okay, Libby. You probably couldn't have stopped it anyway. You can call me Ms. Williams. The divorce is officially final. Although, I'd prefer it if you'd simply call me Nancy. Listen, I'm going to go clear my head and get some coffee. If someone comes in to buy something, offer to order it for them — I guess that's all we can do."

On my way to the coffee shop, I stop in at Ink'd Deep, the local tattoo shop owned by my landlords, to let them know I won't be stopping by at their barbecue tonight because of the calamity at the shop.

I try to sneak in the front door and be unobtrusive, but that's not the way things work around here. Jade, one of the owners, is the first to notice me. "What are you doing here? Didn't you just get out of the hospital? I thought they told you to go home and rest. The flu is killing people. I would've thought over a week in the hospital and being connected to oxygen would have persuaded you not to overdo it," she scolds.

I sway a little on my feet and my vision grays at the edges. I struggle to find the words to explain my actions. "I … I stopped by the shop to pick up some paints to occupy myself because I knew I'd be down for a while — but the whole place is trashed."

I hate feeling weak. I lean against the room divider and try to pretend nothing is wrong, but it's far too late. Marcus and Jett notice my hesitation and come over to help me. Even though they have both been my friends for two years now, I still flinch at their touch. If I was strong enough, I would kick myself for my response. I see a look of surprise and pain across Jett's face. This nearly crushes me. Jett and his wife have been nothing but generous with me. They allow me to live in a house on the property for a pittance for rent. I know it's not even remotely close to market value, but they never say a word. They claim I'm doing them a huge favor by watering the plants and giving their cat food and water while they're gone. Yet, this is how I repay him? I can't believe his presence still makes me jump even after more than two years.

Marcus and Jett escort me back to a large comfortable couch in the break room and help me sit down. Rogue comes in and drapes a blanket over me. Softly she asks, "What's going on, Nancy?"

"Someone demolished the shop while I was in the hospital," I explain. "I don't even know how I can put it all back together before Savannah and Casey come back into town for the holidays. My daughter trusted me to take care of Paint Your Art Out while Casey was going to school. I thought I had it covered. I had a big tole painting workshop planned for Christmas — but I've been so sick, I haven't had a chance to do any promotion for it and now I don't even know if we have the supplies in stock." I start to tear up. "I'm so sorry, I know I shouldn't —"

A distinguished gentleman with silver hair and a sexy smile wearing cargo shorts and with a dramatic tattoo curling around his calf pokes his head in the break room. "Sorry to interrupt, Jett. I need to go. Do you want to run my card now or do you want me to pay when I come back next week?" he asks as he twirls his card between his fingers.

"Sorry to keep you waiting, Rex. I need to swing by your office after we close tonight. I'll talk to you then. You know the routine with your tattoo. Keep it covered and out of the sun," Jett replies. "We don't want those colors fading."

"It's gorgeous work," I stammer and then blush uncontrollably.

Rex looks down at the see-through bandage. "Yeah, it took us a while to get here. I was amazed what Jett could do, considering what a gnarly mess my skin is underneath all this beautiful artwork."

"Really? They can do that?"

He nods and pulls his cargo shorts up to expose more of his thigh. "Believe it or not, the scarring Jett covered up was even more extensive."

Instinctively, I cover my scar on my upper breast with my left hand as I ask, "Looks painful. What hap —" I have to close my eyes as a wave of dizziness overtakes me. I slump back against the cushions of the couch.

Marcus yells out into the shop, "I think Ms. Lyons needs your help, Jade."

Jade rushes in and I mumble, "It's Williams now —
"

"Well, your divorce took just about forever. It should make your life easier. Nancy, do you trust me to take care of you?" Jade asks.

I nod and then instantly regret the motion. "I think so," I respond with a puzzled look.

Something in my expression must've struck Jade as funny because she laughs. "Don't worry, a lot of people feel that way about me. I'll take care of you. It's obvious to everyone except you that you should have stayed in bed today. So, I'm going to make it happen. After all, you need to be strong for the big Christmas get-together." She puts her arm around me and helps me to a standing position.

"Normally, I would resent you all to pieces for your bossiness, but today I'm too sick to care," I admit as I lean on her for support.

# CHAPTER TWO

# REX

I SLIDE THE PAPERWORK across my desk to Jett. "You gotta know I have a million questions about this afternoon. Who is Nancy Williams — and what is she to you?"

For a moment Jett looks confused. "You mean our tenant, Nancy Lyons ... uh ... right ... I forgot. Her divorce came through and she finally gets to dump her albatross."

My eyebrows raise. "I thought you believed in happily ever after and all that jazz."

"I do — unless the guy you're married to is a complete jerk face," Jett responds with a grimace.

"That bad?" I ask.

Jett nods. "I'm sure there's a bunch of stuff she's not telling us, but the things Nancy does admit to are downright horrific. After their son was born with some sort of birth defect, her husband turned into a crazed zealot and took their entire family on the road in search of faith healers. After Owen died, George was afraid they would be charged with the death of their son. He took his wife and ran, leaving their other two children to fend for themselves. He basically kept her hostage and on the run for about fifteen years. They didn't even have a home, and he never allowed her to seek medical help."

"I guess that explains why she looked like you could knock her over with a light summer breeze yesterday. So, you gonna tell me where this loser is? Seems to me, a guy who could treat a woman like that and desert his children needs an attitude adjustment or two."

Jett smirks. "Too late. Georgie boy split town. Seems he couldn't handle it when his wife grew a backbone and stood up for herself. That's why it took so blasted long for her to get a divorce. She had to find the slime ball."

"Wouldn't it simply be a matter of paperwork?"

"That's what her son-in-law Mark, who is an attorney, told her. Even so, she didn't want to take the easy way out. She wanted George to know she wanted the marriage over."

"Wow! That took guts."

"You have no idea. From what I understand, this guy basically ruled everything in her life from what she wore, to what she ate and drank. He even criticized her thoughts."

I shake my head in disbelief. "I don't even pretend to understand how that happens."

"Me neither. You've met my wife and daughter. Can you imagine me telling them what they were allowed to believe or giving them fashion advice? I tried that once when Jade was in junior high school. I swear her skirts got three inches shorter," Jett reminisces with a chuckle.

"So, I guess I have a question. Is there anything we can do to make Nancy's life a little easier and prove to her not all guys are jerks?" I ask as I idly spin a pen between my fingers.

"Funny you should ask. I was thinking about calling an emergency meeting of Coastal Cruisers with a Cause to see if they might want to help. I don't know if you've heard, but Nancy was recently hospitalized with a wicked case of influenza and pneumonia. While she was away, somebody completely trashed her business. She'll need a little help to put it all back together. You met her yesterday — if someone doesn't step in, she'll try to do it herself."

"I did. Although she seems to have the willpower to fight the world, she doesn't seem to have the strength to shadowbox with her own reflection. Let's do this. I'll call the guys."

"Are we sure an isolated tornado didn't go through here?" I ask Jett as I look around the store in dismay. Every place I look, something is overturned or demolished. The stench is something I associate more with a bathroom at a seedy bar than a craft store.

"From what I understand, this was caused by a bunch of twenty-something bridesmaids who had far too much to drink."

"Any reason she doesn't want to file an insurance claim?"

"Knowing Nancy, I suspect she doesn't want it to go back on her kids."

I raise my eyebrow. "I'd definitely bill the delinquents who attended the party."

"Not a bad idea. I'll have the guys keep track of any damaged inventory during cleanup and ask Libby to give me an itemized list. Mark should be able to issue a sufficiently scary letter asking for reimbursement."

Using the box cutter, I break down the last box of many and throw it in the pile out back. As I enter the store, out of the corner of my eye, I see Libby wobble on one of the step stools as she struggles to put inventory away. I rush over to steady her. "Careful there," I caution.

I am about half a beat too slow and Libby falls backwards into my arms. Fortunately, I catch her and set her back on her feet before she drops the merchandise in her hands. She blushes. "I'm so sorry. I guess I'm just not tall enough to do the restocking."

I try to surreptitiously work out a kink in my shoulder. Honestly, it's never been quite the same since the car sideswiped me on the interstate and caused the wipeout which almost ended my ability to ride altogether. "You're welcome. It's not a problem. Is that how everybody has to do inventory?"

She shrugs. "Most of the good storage space is clear up there." Libby says as she points to large cupboards about two feet over her head.

I look around to find Jett. "Hey, did you say Nancy was readmitted to the hospital until Wednesday?"

Jett nods. "Yeah, turns out the pneumonia was a little tougher than they thought."

"Would it be okay if I build her a rolling ladder system?" I ask as I study the shop.

Jett narrows his eyes. "Know anything about that?"

I chuckle at his skepticism. "I wasn't always a banking executive. I worked my way through college as an apprentice to a furniture maker."

"Why would you do this for my boss?" Libby asks in a distrustful voice. "Are you sure you won't charge Nancy anything?"

I shake my head. "Not a dime. Sometimes you just encounter someone who has had so much bad happen in their life, you feel compelled to show them there are still good people in the world. Something tells me Ms. Williams needs to be reminded that good things can happen to good people."

Jett grins. "Amen. Besides, it's the holiday season. Knock yourself out. I'll do my best to keep her out of here until your crew is done. Diamond will be thrilled. My wife already thinks you are one of the nicest guys she's ever met. Wait until she hears about this."

I pull at the neck of my T-shirt and shift my weight uncomfortably. "Let's keep this between us. After all, I'm supposed to be a tough guy — you know, I'm in a motorcycle gang."

Jett scoffs at me. "Yeah, we're in a motorcycle gang which specializes in raising money for children's causes.

I don't think our toughness quotient is off the charts."

"Does my tattoo count?"

Jett claps me on the back of the shoulder. "Yeah, Hudson, you're a real rebel. Don't worry, your secret is safe with me."

Libby makes a show of zipping her lips and goes back to sorting inventory, while I make mental plans to make Ms. William's workplace safer and more beautiful.

# CHAPTER THREE

# NANCY

NERVOUSLY, I FLUFF MY hair and rearrange the couch pillows behind me as Ketki opens the door. I don't know why I'm even worried about all this. If I look as bad as I feel, I'm probably as attractive as a dingy, worn-out dishrag.

Ketki bursts into the living room. Being a teenager hasn't slowed her down much. "Grandma, this guy is here to see you. He says he works at a bank. I told him I'm really good at math and he said I should consider a career in financing."

"That's great, Ki. Maybe you guys can talk about it sometime," I reply.

Just then, I hear a car honk in the distance and Ketki brushes a kiss across my cheek. "Gotta go — but you can't tell Mom and Dad. I'm going Christmas shopping with Maya."

"Call if you need anything," I instruct as I watch my granddaughter rush out the door.

For a moment, I just awkwardly stare at Rex.

"Jett said you wanted me to swing by," he comments, breaking the silence.

I reach over to the TV tray beside me. "Um … I think you left these behind when you were remodeling my shop."

He takes the glasses from me. "Oh, I must've dropped these the day when I caught Libby. I drove myself crazy trying to find them. These are my computer glasses."

I shoot him a puzzled glance. "You're remodeling the whole shop simply because Libby almost fell down?"

He looks profoundly disappointed by my question. Instantly, I wonder what I've done to disappoint him. "I was hoping to surprise you," he explains. "Who spilled the beans?"

"One of our regular suppliers was visiting his mom in the hospital and happened to walk by my room. He stopped in for a brief chat and complimented me on all the improvements to my store. Imagine how awkward it was when I didn't know there had been any improvements. Last I knew, poor Libby was trying to manage the chaos with just a broom, a dustpan, and a little Windex."

Rex looks a little uncomfortable. "I'm sorry. I never meant to embarrass you. It started out as a simple cleanup project to help you deal with the mess the hooligans left behind. One thing led to another and soon it grew into a competition to try to fix anything which might be causing you difficulty at the shop. You know how it gets with us guys. We try to one up each other when it comes to how creative we can be with our projects. It was a blast. I love woodworking projects and since I don't get to do things with my hands in my job, I guess I got a little carried away. I hope you like what I've done. I didn't mean to take over your shop, honest."

Tears threaten as I look at him and search his face. "You barely know me. We only talked for a few minutes the other day. I might be mistaken because things are a little fuzzy from that day. I was really sick — but the only reason I know your last name at all, is because you had a business card stuck in your glasses case. Otherwise I would've had to call Jade to figure out who you are. Why would you go out of your way to help somebody like me? Do you even know my name?"

"Yes, I know your name, Nancy Williams. I know your friends speak very highly of you. I know you have worked yourself to the point of utter exhaustion trying to keep your daughter's business afloat. I understand you're operating with a part-time staff and a shoestring budget so your daughter could move to California to be with her husband while he attends college. That's admirable and hard as heck. It takes courage and guts. I just wanted to help you out."

I sigh and cover my face with my hands before a fresh round of rib-splitting coughs overtakes me. Once I can catch my breath, I reply, "I love my new friends over at Ink'd Deep, but they really need to learn the definition of 'private conversation'."

Rex chuckles. "I know what you mean. They put a whole new spin on the phrase 'community involvement'. Honestly I don't know what I would do without them."

"So, you're more than a client of Ink'd Deep, too?"

"I started out as Jett's client, but over the years I'd like to think we've become close friends. He and Diamond helped me cope with the loss of my fiancé and I was there with them when their son Onyx committed suicide."

I swallow hard. "Your life is never the same when you lose a child."

"I agree. When someone you love dies, it changes you. Jett told me about Owen. I'm sorry for your loss."

I wipe away tears. "Thank you. I'm just lucky my beautiful daughters have the grace to still speak to me. I know I probably deserved much less."

Rex leans over and pats my leg. "Sometimes, there are miracles lurking where you least expect them. When you're feeling better and want to see what Jett and his gang have been up to, let me know. I'd love to play tour guide."

My heart speeds up when he touches me — not from fear and queasiness as it did in the last few years I was with George, but rather, it's an odd sense of giddiness. It's like the warm sense of anticipation I felt in junior high when I found out the cutest kid in class had a crush on me.

I have to clear my throat before I muster the courage to blurt, "I'd love that."

# CHAPTER FOUR

# REX

I FEEL RIDICULOUS AS I drive the large Lincoln to Nancy's home. Even so, I chose it because it has so many more creature comforts than my beat up old pickup or my motorcycle. Although Florida doesn't get bone-chillingly cold this time of year, it would probably be best if Nancy doesn't get chilled at all, given her fragile medical state. Besides, heated leather seats never hurt anyone this time of year. I grab the roses from the back seat and straighten my tie as I walk up the path to the little cottage behind Jett and Diamond's house.

When Nancy opens the door, she scrutinizes me from head to toe. "Oh dear! Obviously, I'm underdressed for wherever we're going," she says as she turns away. When I reach out to stop her, she flinches.

I draw my hand back as I explain, "No, wait! It's me who's overdressed. I just came from work and I haven't had a chance to change my clothes yet. You look beautiful."

Nancy looks down at herself. "It's only a turtleneck and jeans — beautiful might be a bit of a stretch." She grabs her purse and coat. She seems a little befuddled when I offer to help her put it on. Nancy gives a happy little shrug and allows me to help her. Her eyes widen after she finishes locking up the house and sees the car. "Why are we taking a limo just to go see the shop?"

"This isn't really a limo. This is my company car — actually that's not quite true. This is the car we use when we want to schmooze other bank executives."

Nancy looks at me blankly. "Why?"

A burst of laughter erupts from me. "You know, that's a good question. I'm not sure what it accomplishes. I guess it's just tradition."

"George didn't trust banks. When Savannah gave me the job at Paint Your Art Out, Shelby had to teach me how to use a bank again. I hadn't used one since my daughters were teeny. I didn't even know what an ATM card was."

"Seriously? It might simply be an occupational hazard, but I can't imagine living in a world without banks. How could you even pay your bills in today's world of computerized everything?"

"We didn't have any bills. George did everything in his power to make me and the kids absolutely invisible. We weren't on anyone's radar."

I glance over at her and take in her beautiful, platinum blonde hair sprinkled through with gray, her pale blue eyes and engaging smile. "I find it hard to believe you wouldn't stand out from the crowd anytime, anywhere — but that's just me."

Nancy reaches out and runs her fingers across mine

in the lightest of strokes. "Thank you. You really know how to make me feel like a million bucks."

Together, we walk up to Nancy's storefront. I move behind her and ask her to close her eyes. "Believe me, it will be worth it."

"I won't be able to see anything, and I'll probably trip over something and fall. I can't afford to land in the hospital again," she points out logically.

"Trust me, I'll protect you and keep you safe."

Nancy stiffens and crosses her arms around her waist. "It's nothing personal, Rex — but these days, I find it hard to trust anyone. I don't think I ever will."

I resist the urge to reach up and wipe the stress lines from her brow. "Hopefully, my friends and I will help restore your faith in humanity."

I take the keys from her trembling hand and open the shop, flipping the lights on as the melodic chimes sound, announcing our arrival.

For a moment, she simply stands at the front of her store and turns in a wide circle as she takes everything in. She gasps softly before she turns back and bolts into my arms. She throws her arms around my neck and squeezes me tight.

"Thank you so much. This is perfect. It's right out of my dreams. I used to hang out at a library with strikingly similar ladders. I dreamed one day I would have a library in my own home filled with bookcases from floor-to-ceiling with ladders just like that." She pauses for a moment to wipe away tears with a crumpled Kleenex. "I know Savannah's store isn't really my home, but it's become the closest thing to a home I could ever have."

Instinctively, I place my arms around her waist. "I'm glad you like it," I say as I swallow a lump in my throat.

"I still don't understand why you would do something like this for me," she protests.

Remembering my manners, I step back and place my arms at my side. "Once when I was just a little boy, my father was drunk — like he often was — and he set fire to our house while he was working on a car in the garage. Of course, he didn't remember the whole thing, but if it hadn't been for the kindness of strangers, we would have been homeless."

"That's awful, I'm so sorry. It must've been hard on you as a child."

"Though it was hard in the beginning, it turned out to be a blessing in disguise. My mom, who had never worked outside the home a day in her life, ended up working for, and then owning, a successful chain of daycare centers. Helping her with the books is what got me started on a career in finance."

"There's nothing like a disaster to wake you up and get you started on the right path. I learned my lesson the hard way," she comments with a haunted look.

My cell phone vibrates in my pocket. I pull it out and read the message. I grimace and let out a heavy sigh as I realize the implications. I glance up at Nancy. "I'm so sorry. Something has come up at work. I can drop you back at your place or swing by later to pick you up, if you'd like."

"You've already done far too much. I was supposed to meet my daughter, Shelby, for lunch anyway. I'll just have her come here. I want her to see all of this. It's like a holiday miracle. I can't thank you enough."

"I was honored to pay it forward. Enjoy." With a great sense of regret, I turn and walk away.

# Chapter Five

# Nancy

"Libby, when you have a moment, can you go outside and see if this display is straight? I can never tell from in here," I yell across the store as I try to arrange items in the window display.

Just then, the chimes on the door ring. An older lady and a young girl in a wheelchair come through the door followed by an older gentleman.

The little girl makes a beeline toward all the beading sets while the older woman focuses on the stained-glass pieces. The gentleman seems really focused on the ceramic items we have available for painting. He looks up at the woman he came in with. "Gwendolyn, come look at these. They're great. Aidan should get several for his day camp. They would make great souvenirs for the kids to take home."

"You know, that's not such a bad idea," she answers. "Maybe we should have Maddie make one to commemorate her trip to Disney World. Aidan would love it. They even have coffee mugs. You know how much coffee that man drinks. Madeleine, let's go see what Papa wants."

The little girl pushes her wheelchair over to the ceramic display. "May I paint one?"

Gwendolyn picks up a box and studies it. Sadly, she shakes her head. "I'm sorry Maddie, this says it would take too long to dry. We have to leave for the airport in a couple of hours."

I put the window decorations down and walk over to my customers. "I'm sorry, I couldn't help but overhear. I'm Nancy. Do you have a few minutes to hang around a bit?"

"Hi Nancy, I'm Denny and this is my wife, Gwendolyn, and our grand-god-daughter Maddie. We're from Oregon and we just came to visit Disney World." He looks at his watch. "We have a little while before we have to go to the airport."

"It turns out my display piece recently got broken. Would you like to paint another one for me?" I ask Maddie.

She nods eagerly.

"I'll send you pictures when it's finished processing." I hand Denny a piece of paper. "If you write down your contact information and the piece of pottery you want to order, I'll send you one. That way you won't need to worry about protecting it on the flight. I can give you a discount for your trouble."

"Oh, please don't bother," Gwendolyn insists. "I own a small floral business. I know what it's like. You just charge us your normal price, please. Your shop is delightful, and I love all the tole paintings. I wish we lived closer because I'd love to take classes. I've always wanted to learn how to do it, but I'm intimidated."

As I set out the painting materials for Madeleine and slide a plastic apron over her head, I say, "It's funny you should ask. I had great plans for a class to make beautiful Christmas decorations. Then, life derailed my plans in a big way and I ended up in the hospital. So far, I haven't figured out how to make up for the time I lost." I place paint on a palette for Maddie. I look down at her and instruct, "I have enough brushes. You can use a different brush for each color. You may use all the colors or only a few. It's up to you."

"Can I paint a Christmas tree? You don't have any trees in Florida like we have in Oregon. Your trees look funny here."

"I agree. Palm trees are different. I think a Christmas tree would be perfect."

After Maddie has been painting quietly for a couple of minutes, Gwendolyn asks, "Have you ever thought about offering your classes online?"

I let loose with a peal of laughter. "I'm sorry, you don't know me well enough to understand how funny your suggestion is. I barely know how to turn a computer on. There's no way I could offer a class over the computer. I still struggle to use my cell phone."

Denny chuckles. "I used to be the same way. But my grandson set me straight. He is a whiz at these things. He is like a social media guru."

"My husband is not exaggerating. Our grandson started creating anime when he was in junior high school. He's even had some of his work featured on television. Anyway, he does amazing things on YouTube. He convinced me to do a floral arranging class on YouTube. It wasn't nearly as difficult as I thought it might be. Actually, it was fun."

"Pardon me for asking, but can you make any money that way?" I press, trying not to sound rude.

"Oh yes! People ordered supplies directly from my shop. Denny and I shipped a supply box and there was an enrollment fee. We were able to reach far more people than we would have ever fit in my little store."

"Do you think I have time? It's already the first week of November. I was planning to hold the class during the second week of December."

Denny grimaces. "That might be a little tight. Let me talk to Gabriel about the camera equipment you'll need. I might contact one of my friends here locally. Tristan will be able to hook you up with a local supplier for the camera equipment. He does all sorts of surveillance stuff through his company, Identity Bank — he knows his camera equipment."

"Tristan Macklin?" I ask, as my jaw goes slack. "You mean the one married to Rogue, the tattoo artist?"

Denny nods. "Yeah, you know them?"

"Yes, they are my friends and Rogue's boss is my landlord."

"Well, this is one of those small world moments, for sure. It will certainly make things easier. Gabriel can just tell Tristan what he uses for his YouTube set up and Tristan can get one of the teenagers from his gaming clubs to help you set it up and give you a hand with the social media piece."

"I don't know why I didn't think of it. My granddaughter, Ketki, knows all about that stuff. She is forever telling me about Facebook, Instagram, and Snapchat. I bet she'd be thrilled to help me."

Maddie gingerly holds up the plate she's been painting. "I can help too, see?"

"You sure can. If I ever get all this organized, I'd love to have you help me teach a class on painting. You did a great job."

"We'd love to come back," Gwendolyn says with a sigh. "Unfortunately, we need to go. Here is my phone number. Please call me, I would like to put you in touch with my grandson. I think it would be phenomenal if you could share your shop with people on the Internet. I would love to take classes from you."

"Thanks for giving me the push I needed to put myself out there. You'll never know how much it means to me," I say as I hand Gwendolyn a business card with my cell number on the back. "I hope I really do see you in my classes."

Gwendolyn smiles up at Denny. "I know exactly what you mean. I had someone who believed in me when I was too frightened to believe in myself. I know it can make a world of difference. Just know you have fans in Oregon who are rooting for you. Good luck with everything."

As I watch the family leave the shop, I can barely contain my excitement as my mind is whirling with dozens of new ideas.

"Okay Grandma, I set up a Facebook page for Paint Your Art Out. It automatically links to the Instagram and Pinterest accounts I set up for the business. I talked to Gabriel, and he sent schematics over for me to set up all the cameras in your workspace for the class. What a cool guy! It's too bad he's too busy to play video games. Are you ready to send the message?"

"What message?" I ask, feeling a bit lost. All this computer talk still sounds like gibberish.

Ketki looks exasperated. "Grandma, we talked about this. You need to send a Christmas message to all your fans to let them know about the class and to invite them to subscribe to your YouTube channel."

"Do I actually have fans?"

"We're working on it. Lots of people like you, Grandma. They think what you do is neat. We had a few flyers made up and they're planning to put them out at the coffee shop next door. Of course, Jade will put them out at Ink'd Deep. I'm sure if people hear about the class, they'll be interested. Having a presence on social media will help."

"Do you really think so?" I ask skeptically. "I'm simply a nobody who teaches a painting class. I'm not anybody famous."

"But you're talented, interesting to listen to, and really smart. I think you will make a good teacher. I bet other people will think so too. As soon as I have the camera equipment set up, I think you should make a video telling people why they should take your class," Ketki suggests.

"I guess I have nothing to lose. Jett and his friends spent a lot of time and effort fixing this place up. The least I can do is put it to good use. If you need me, I'll be in the restroom trying to make myself presentable and having a little mini-meltdown as I try not to have a panic attack."

"I am not worried. You're just like Savannah and Shelby. You've been through much tougher stuff. When things get hard, you just buckle down and do what needs to be done."

I smile at my granddaughter. "I think that might be the nicest thing anyone has ever said to me."

Ketki grins at me. "Thank you. I try. A lot of people say I'm just like you."

# Chapter Six

# Rex

Jett wipes the excess ink off my tattoo as he finishes up the touch up work. "So, how are things going with Nancy?"

"What do you mean? I finished up the job at her shop weeks ago. I showed you the pictures, remember?"

"Yeah, you absolutely killed it on the woodworking. I just figured you'd use it as your excuse to start things, not end them," Jett suggests with a shrug.

I lift myself up off the tattoo table and tuck in my shirt. "You know, it is possible to be nice and not expect anything in return," I respond with more than a hint of sarcasm.

"True enough. Few people actually are," he counters.

"Bingo! You made my argument for me. That's exactly why I should walk away. She expects to have to repay me," I reply stubbornly.

"You've been alone a long time Rex. I haven't seen you this interested in someone in years. Do you really want to walk away?"

I stuff my hands in my pocket. "Honestly? It's the last thing I want to do. But … what's done is done."

Jett reaches behind him and pulls his laptop off the counter. He brings his Facebook page up and shows me something in his feed. "What if I told you 'done' isn't really done?"

"What you mean?"

Jett nods toward the page. "Nancy is holding a class. She's broadcasting it all over the web. She's nervous no one will show up, so she wants a few friendly faces there. You in?"

"What kind of class?"

"I don't know, read the post, man! It's some sort of Christmas message asking for support from her friends. She invited all of us. Diamond and Jade are totally jazzed. My daughter insists this class will help my tattoo work. I don't know if she's right — but Nancy is in a tight spot, so I figure it's for a good cause. If you go, I won't be the only dude in the class."

I shrug. "Works for me."

Jett laughs out loud. "For a guy with such strong moral principles, you sure caved mighty quick."

I sigh. "I don't know what it is about the lovely Ms. Williams. I can't seem to stop thinking about her. From the second I walked out of her store, I regretted my decision. Maybe this is my chance to have a do-over."

"Stranger things have been known to happen around here."

Her beauty takes my breath away for a moment as I walk into the classroom. I thought Nancy was pretty the first time I saw her, but that version of her was like a faded watercolor painting compared to the vivacious woman standing at the front of her store engaging with her students. Her eyes are sparkling, and her smile is wide as she laughs. Her granddaughter is busy clipping a microphone to her bright red shirt and straightening her black apron embellished with a jaunty candy cane.

After Ketki has Nancy all hooked up, Ketki runs and turns on the lights and cameras. I watch with concern as Nancy takes a deep breath and swallows hard — but she pulls it together and turns and faces the class. "Welcome to Paint Your Art Out. My name is Nancy Williams. Tonight, I'll be teaching you about the joy of tole painting and how you can use it to brighten up your holidays. Tole painting is great because you don't have to have any special equipment and you can paint on almost anything. You can recycle old gardening equipment like watering cans and flowerpots, picture frames, doorknobs or Christmas ornaments, which is what we will be doing tonight. You can breathe new life into found objects and make them beautiful again. All it takes is a little elbow grease, creativity and run-of-the-mill acrylic paints and brushes."

Nancy looks out at the audience and shows us all a collection of brushes and a few tubes of acrylic paint. I can tell when her eyes meet mine because her smile falters and she frowns. She takes a few moments to collect herself and continues speaking. "Tole painting isn't intended to be perfect. It's meant to be a fun way to add color to the world around you."

Nancy's eyes briefly meet mine once more. After that, she studiously ignores me. I can't help but feel a little deflated. This is not at all how I envisioned this scenario in my head. I didn't exactly expect a parade, but I thought she would at least be happy to see me. I guess I should have followed my first instincts and left her well enough alone. I suppose I better stick around and explain myself. Although honestly, I don't know what to say exactly. I am not sure why I came tonight. The only answer I can come up with is that walking away from Nancy Williams isn't an outcome I feel comfortable with. So, even if I make a fool out of myself, I want to get to know her.

# CHAPTER SEVEN

# NANCY

AFTER WHAT SEEMED LIKE forever, the class is finally over. I can't tell you how it went or even what I said. My brain was on autopilot and it was like an out-of-body experience. The students seemed to respond okay, and they didn't seem lost. Many of them painted cute designs on the balsa wood ornaments and they seemed thrilled with what they created. Even my granddaughter had nothing critical to say about my delivery and she seemed all smiles as she put away the equipment and left the shop with a few of her friends. Eventually after I've put away all the supplies and cleaned my shop within an inch of its life, I know I've run out of excuses. I need to deal with Rex Hudson.

I could pretend I don't know he's standing quietly over by the cash register simply waiting for me to expend my frenetic energy like a child who's had too much birthday cake. But the only person I'm fooling is me. I am hyper aware of every breath the man takes. It's almost as if I can feel his presence on a molecular level. I gather my courage and ask, "Why are you here?"

"You asked me to be," Rex answers simply.

My eyes widen. "I did?"

"That's the way I read it." He shrugs. "I read your Christmas message. You said you needed the support of your friends to help make your class a success. I consider you my friend, so I came."

I'm so shocked, I have to remember to close my mouth.

"What's that look for?" Rex asks with a puzzled glance.

"Oh, I don't know," I answer sarcastically. "Maybe it's because you walked out of my store one day for a business meeting and I didn't hear from you for weeks. I know you know where I work and where I live and even have my phone number because you sent me a text message. You know who my landlords are. You even know who my friends are. So why would I have any reason to believe you are my friend?"

Rex physically recoils from my words. "Fair enough. You're right. Walking out of your shop was one of the hardest things I've ever done — although I had a legitimate reason to leave. I don't know if you've been watching the news, but one of my employees decided they weren't getting paid enough and that they should receive extra compensation by skimming off money from the safe deposit boxes. The day I left your shop was the day we discovered the thefts."

I wince. "Maybe my ex-husband wasn't so wrong about banks after all." I quip.

"From what I understand, your ex-husband was

wrong about an awful lot of things — the intrinsic corruption of all bankers notwithstanding. The point is we caught the theft and returned all the missing money. Actually, that's a misstatement; it's not really the point I was trying to make."

I raise my eyebrow as an unspoken challenge.

Rex runs his hand through his hair and shifts his position against the wall. "Look, I'm not great at all this stuff. In case you haven't noticed, I tend to stick my foot in my mouth a lot. What I meant to say is I fervently wish I hadn't had to take off that day. I was enjoying my time with you. You are the most interesting person I've met in years. I wanted to come back and spend time with you."

"So, why didn't you? I thought I had done something wrong," I confess.

"I didn't want to be dishonest. I told you I worked on your shop as a gift. I didn't want you to feel like I was expecting something in exchange for doing the work on your shop."

I'm silent for a few moments as his words sink in — but even as they do, they still don't make much sense.

"So, you let me think you hated me because you didn't want me to think friendship was a two-way street?"

"Well, when you put it in those terms, it doesn't make much sense. It was much clearer in my head. I guess I was trying to do you a favor without you feeling like you had to pay me back."

I choke back a snort of laughter. "As if I could! The

work you and Jett, together with all your friends, did in my shop would've cost me thousands of dollars. Rex, you guys made me custom furniture and a storage system. The cleanup work alone would've cost far more than I could ever afford — let alone pay back. It's like you explained about your mom. Someday, I might be in a position where I get to pay it forward to someone else."

"I know you are the type of person who would do exactly that."

I blush a little before I add, "I have to tell you something else. I wanted you to come back and talk to me. I waited for you. It had nothing to do with the beautiful furniture and cabinetry you made for me."

Rex clears his throat nervously. "It didn't?"

I shake my head. "Nope. For the first time in years I was having a conversation with a man who was listening attentively to every word I said and respecting my input. You didn't belittle me or tell me I didn't have the right to think my thoughts or disagree with you. It was astounding. I haven't felt so empowered in a long time."

Rex hangs his head. "Now I feel even more terrible about the way I left and didn't come back. Do you suppose there's any way we can start over?"

I grow pensive. "I don't know. I'm afraid to make any snap judgments. Let me think about it for a bit. I still have your number in my phone. I'll call you after I've processed it all. This whole day has been completely overwhelming."

"Mom, why do you look so upset? I thought the class was a huge success. Nearly everyone I spoke to said they wanted to sign up for more classes. The reviews I read online indicated everybody loved it."

I shrug. "It's not really that. The class went better than I could've expected, I suppose. I don't remember much. I was so nervous I couldn't even feel my lips moving."

"Then what's the problem?" Shelby asks.

"I can't figure out why Rex was there." I blurt.

"Rex?" she asks.

"Rex Hudson, He's the guy who built all the cabinetry and the ladders, so I can properly store inventory at the shop."

"Why wouldn't he be? You invited all your friends. I saw the Facebook message."

"You sound like him! That's exactly what he said."

Shelby raises an eyebrow. "What's the problem? You've never been one to discriminate on gender. You encouraged Mark to take up painting to relieve his work stress."

"You're right. It's not because he's a man — well, not exactly." I throw my hands up in the air. "Or maybe it is. I don't know what my problem is. Rex is such a handsome man. I guess I was afraid he would be like your dad and second-guess everything I did and call my work worthless. I didn't want to let him mean a lot in my life. I suppose I was right to be cautious. I mean, the last time I saw Rex, he took a phone call and walked right out of my life."

"You had a good time when he was in your life, right? So… you wouldn't object if he walked back into it, would you?" Shelby presses.

I reach up and brush my bangs out of my eyes. "I have the best time when Rex is around," I confess candidly. "Honestly, I don't think I would mind a bit if he walked right through the front door."

Shelby smiles slyly. "Well, Mom, you have a proven strategy. It worked once, maybe it'll work again. Send the man a Christmas message — a personal invitation to Christmas dinner would be perfect."

# Chapter Eight

# Rex

I have to blink, not once but twice, when Nancy's name comes up on my Facebook page. Not only has she sent me a friend request, but this personal message seems to be an invitation to Christmas dinner at her house. I breathe a sigh of relief. When she didn't call after the painting class, I thought I had blown my second chance too.

I pull out my cell phone and call one of the classiest people I know. "Hey, Diamond, do you mind if I pick your brain about something?"

"I guess not. Although I guess it depends on the subject matter," she answers with a laugh.

"I haven't done this dating thing for a very long time and I don't want to screw it up. I've been invited to Nancy's house for Christmas dinner. What should I bring?"

"Did your invitation specify anything?" Diamond asks.

"No, that would be why I called you for guidance,"

I tease.

"I don't think I would bring food. She probably has had her menu planned for a while. I don't think you could go wrong with a houseplant though."

"Perfect. I noticed she had a lot of African violets."

"Well, there you go. If you really want to pull out the big guns and impress her, make sure you roll up your sleeves and help her with the dishes when dinner is over."

"I thought all gentlemen knew to step up," I reply.

"Only the smart ones." Diamond chuckles. "Seriously, go and have a good time. Nancy needs a guy like you in her life. Merry Christmas, Rex. You need somebody like Nancy in your life too."

You would think age would make this dating thing a little easier. Instead, I think I'm more nervous than I was as a teenager. At least when I was younger, I didn't understand what was at stake. I had an undeniable swagger I seem to be missing these days.

I shift the potted plant into my other hand and brush some invisible lint off my jacket. I rock nervously on the balls of my feet as I stand on the front porch of the neatly-kept little mother-in-law-cottage and wait for the door to open.

When it opens, I encounter a younger version of Nancy with pale blonde curly hair. "Oh ... umm. Mom didn't mention you were so handsome. Hi! I'm

Savannah. I can't tell you how much I appreciate what you did at Paint Your Art Out. I always had huge plans for my shop and then life got in the way. Even so, my dreams never even touched what you accomplished. It's beautiful. Thank you so much for rescuing Mom."

"Honestly, it was my pleasure. I haven't had a chance to work on a project like yours in years. It was fun to brush off my creative side for a while."

Savannah yells over her shoulder, "Mom! Your hunk is here."

It's been years since I've blushed as red as a stop sign, but apparently, I'm still capable of that too.

Ketki stares at her in amazement. "Wow — Aunt Savannah! Usually people say I talk before I think, but even I wouldn't embarrass Grandma like that."

Nancy rushes to the door. Ignoring the drama between her daughter and granddaughter, she spies the flowers I'm awkwardly holding in my hands. "Oh, how lovely! You didn't have to — but I'm glad you did. They're beautiful. Come on in. We're about to sit down for dinner. This is my daughter Savannah, and her husband Casey. The guy over there with dark hair is Shelby's husband Mark, and Shelby is helping me in the kitchen. I think you've already met Ketki. She is Mark and Shelby's daughter. If you'll excuse me, I need to get the rest of the food ready. Dinner will be out shortly."

Mark comes over to shake my hand. "What did you think of my mother-in-law's painting class? When she first turned me onto it, I was skeptical. But I've become a big fan. It's a really relaxing hobby."

"I had a great time. Nancy's a natural born teacher."

Casey comes over and shakes my hand. "You know, I've always thought the same thing. She makes beautiful jewelry boxes too. I've always told her she should teach beginning woodworking classes for women. It would be very empowering."

"That would be phenomenal. A lot of women I know are scared to use power tools. It would be great for them to see someone like Nancy being comfortable using them."

Mark catches Casey's eye and nods. At my quizzical look Casey explains, "After all Nancy's been through, she needs someone who believes in her and her abilities. Basically, she needs someone who is the 'anti-George'. By all appearances, you seem to fit the bill perfectly."

Nancy comes back into the room carrying a large turkey on a platter. She studies our expressions. "From the looks on your faces, I'm not even sure if I want to know what you've been talking about."

Mark winks at his mother-in-law. "For now, I'm going to classify it as need to know. Right now, you don't need to know, and we need to eat." He leans over and kisses his mother-in-law on the cheek. "Trust me Nancy, we love you and would do nothing to hurt you."

I set my fork down after eating the last bite of my cranberry apple tart. "Nancy, this is the best food I've had in I can't remember when. I have to eat in a lot of fancy restaurants as part of my job, but none of them compare to the quality of the food you served today.

Thank you for inviting me for dinner." I take the napkin off my lap and set it on the table. I stand up and collect the dirty dishes and stack them up to take them into the kitchen.

Suddenly, I'm aware of the stillness that has overtaken the room. Everyone is watching Nancy intently. As I look around the room, I notice Mark and Casey exchanging amused looks. I freeze in place waiting for something to happen because I'm not sure what's going on. Finally, Nancy voices her concerns. "What are you doing, Rex?"

I look down at the dishes in front of me. "Getting ready to help you do the dishes," I reply, as I resume gathering plates.

A look of shock mixed with amazement and horror crosses Nancy's face. "But … but it's woman's work," she stammers.

I grin. "Not in my world. I was washing dishes beside my mama as soon as I was tall enough to stand on a chair. My mama would skin me alive if she heard me tell a woman it was her job to wash dishes. In our house, when we ate, everybody washed dishes."

Nancy's eyes widen. "It doesn't make you mad?"

"No, why would it? I like to eat. That means I gotta fix my food and clean up afterwards. Just for the record, I wash my own clothes too."

Savannah can't hold back her laughter anymore. "See Mom? We told you Dad and Reverend Pratchett were crazier than loons. There were no prophecies involved in their teachings. They were simply lazy. There are good men everywhere who don't mind pulling their own weight. They don't make a habit of belittling the women in their lives. It sounds like we've found three of the best. Why don't we retire to the living room and let them clean up this mess while I tell you about what I've been doing in California, and you can catch me up on what's been happening at the shop?"

Nancy is quiet for a few moments before she responds to Savannah's suggestion. "In a minute — but I need to say something to Rex first." She turns to me and urges me to sit back down. "I've been totally unfair to you. I'm sorry. I guess I'm not finding it as easy to be unmarried as I thought it would be. George has been in my life since we were teenagers. I underestimated how much of me he changed. I thought I was finding myself again — you know, the me who I was before him. I'm afraid there's not much of the original Nancy left. If you'll be patient with me, I'd like to try to find the fiercely independent, confident woman I once was."

I reach out and grasp her hands. "Nancy, not a single thing in my life has ever turned out the way I expected it to. Eventually, I just learned to let go and embrace the journey. I'd like to go on that journey with you."

"Really? I'm not sure we'll always make progress," she cautions.

"That's okay. Half the fun is forging a whole new path when the one you thought you were going to take is blocked. How do you feel about starting tomorrow? I have the day off. Have you ever ridden a motorcycle?"

Nancy's eyes widen, and I can see the pulse race at her temple.

"No, but I've always wanted to," she responds with a spark of interest in her eyes.

"Perfect! I love making dreams come true."

# CHAPTER NINE

# NANCY

"Okay, you can turn around now," Jade says as she zips up the jacket.

I pivot around and look at myself in the full-length mirror. My jaw drops open in shock. I can't believe the image staring back at me. Jade has decked me out in black leather with bright blue accents. Even my pants are leather. I look like a cover model for a biker magazine. Reverend Pratchett would definitely not approve of this look.

"I can't believe you just had this stuff lying around," I comment as I twirl in front of the mirror again. "Are you sure these pants aren't too tight?"

Jade shakes her head. "I've been riding forever. I've got riding gear in tons of sizes. They are supposed to be snug. They are not too tight. They look perfect. Just because you like to dress in baggy clothes does not mean you don't have a nice figure under all those layers. You look phenomenal. Do you want me to take you out on the back of my bike, so you can get a feel for it before you go out with Rex?"

45

"No thanks. Ketki bookmarked a few videos on YouTube for me and I studied them last night. I think I understand the basic concept. Besides, it will give me a fantastic excuse to hold on tight."

"That's my girl!" Jade exclaims as she laughs out loud. "You guys have fun. Remember to lean when he leans."

"That actually sounds like solid dating advice too."

Jade brushes her fingers over her wedding ring. "You're right — it is. You have to work together to navigate the tough stuff or you'll crash and burn."

I heave a heavy sigh. "I wish I could've done that with George. But it's hard to support someone who doesn't even see you as a real person."

Jade stands up, walks over and gives me a hug. "Oh Nancy, I didn't mean it like that. You can't be expected to support someone like George. He had no idea what it meant to be a true partner. I know it won't be like that with Rex. He has been around my family for almost as long as I can remember. He knows what it's like to be a true friend in good times and in bad. He'll have your back always. You can count on him."

I shoot her a wry grin. "I hope so. I'm about to get on a fancy bicycle with him and hurl down the highway at ungodly speeds."

Jade smirks at me. "I have a hunch about you. I think you have a hidden wild side and as soon as you get the hang of riding, you'll be as addicted as the rest of us."

"I don't know if I'd go quite that far yet. I just hope

I survive my first date," I reply as I check my lipstick one last time.

My nerves are shot. I can't calmly wait in the house so I'm pacing the width of my porch as I wait for Rex to arrive. I cannot believe I'm going on a date at my age. My oldest daughter is nearly forty. I must be crazy. What does a successful man like Rex want with a woman like me anyway? Even though I've been reintegrating myself into regular society for a few years now after having wandered around the country like a homeless nomad for decades, most days I still feel inadequate to cope with life. I'm not sure what makes me think I'm ready to make a leap quite this large. Without my friends around to cheer me on, this move seems way beyond my grasp.

Just as I'm ready to chicken out and send Rex a message politely begging off, I hear his motorcycle roaring up the street. The urge to flee is strong. Then I remember I'm done running. I've been there, done that — and I'm tired. I lost an incalculable amount of my dignity, self-respect and sense of who I am the last time someone convinced me to run. I'm not about to make those same mistakes again simply because I'm afraid. I try to remember the breathing techniques Diamond and I learned in the yoga class we took.

I breathe deeply and let it out. Gathering my nerve, I watch as Rex pulls up in my driveway on his chopper. He is so strikingly handsome he reminds me of the cowboys in the Westerns my mom used to watch when I was growing up.

Almost without conscious thought I rush off the porch to greet him. When he sees me, a slow grin of appreciation crosses his lips. "I can see you are ready for this adventure. You look stunning. I would be happy to have you on my bike any day of the week."

Rex puts his bike kickstand down and gets off. He reaches out and cups the side of my face as he pulls me closer. "I was going to wait a little longer to do this, but I've thought of little else since the night I got your Christmas message."

The heat in his eyes makes my heart beat faster. "Thinking about what?" I ask breathlessly.

"This —" Rex says as he leans down and brushes a kiss across my lips.

It's been so long since I've felt the loving touch of another, my body doesn't quite know how to react. At first, I freeze. I attempt to relax into his touch and cuddle closer into his chest.

"Mmm … Good morning to you too," I murmur. "I could get used to greetings like that."

Rex grins. "You can tell me that all day, every day. I'd be happy to oblige."

I feel my face grow hot. "Um … let's see how today goes first, okay? It's my first date since high school. I'm a little nervous and I'll probably say a bunch of stuff I probably shouldn't."

"Relax Nancy. I'm hardly in a position to judge. I go

out on a lot of dates only because I'm expected to —
you know, silver fox, eligible bachelor and all. But,
you're the first person I've dated who has mattered in a
very long time. So, I'm just as nervous as you are."

"Why aren't you married with a couple of kids?
What's wrong with you?" I blurt before I remember to
phrase my question like a lady.

The corner of Rex's mouth quirks up. "Oh, I'm sure
there's plenty wrong with me. But I don't know how
much of that is the reason behind my marital status.
Remember when I told you nothing much in my life
goes according to plan? It's especially true when it
comes to relationships. I had planned to be married a
long time ago. Unfortunately, the Oklahoma City
bombing blew those plans to smithereens."

"What do you mean? Was your girlfriend one of the
victims?"

Rex nods. "In a roundabout way — Kelly Anne was
a CNA who was training to be a nurse. During all the
chaos of the bombing, she was pressed into service
trying to save all the victims. She just wouldn't quit
working. She worked around the clock for weeks. She
felt guilty every time she lost a patient. Eventually, the
fatigue and the sense of helplessness got to her, and she
committed suicide."

As his words sink in, I draw in a deep breath. "Oh,
Rex — I'm so sorry. I don't even know how you recover
from something like that."

"I don't know either. For a long time, I blamed

myself. I asked myself questions — like why didn't I see it coming and demand she get help?" Rex swallows hard and rests his chin on the top of my head as he hugs me.

"Finally, I realized even Kelly Anne, who had medical training, couldn't recognize the risk her illness posed. It took me a long time to forgive both of us. By the time I finally got around to doing that, there wasn't anyone special in my life until you."

I lift my head up and kiss the underside of his jaw. "I'm sorry we both had to go through so much pain to get to this point."

Rex returns my kiss. As he pulls away, he says, "Me too. What do you say we trade our painful pasts in for a little time on the open road? I think it's time we left our pain in the rear-view mirror. There is a long road to love. I'm excited to go on this journey with you."

"That's the best idea I've heard all day," I respond.

Rex helps me onto the bike and as he releases the kickstand and pulls out of the driveway, he turns his head and says, "Whatever you do, lean with me."

I rest my cheek against his warm, strong back as I smile. "That was always the plan."

# EPILOGUE

# REX

I TUCK A HIBISCUS flower behind Nancy's left ear and kiss her tenderly. "Are you sure everyone will be okay with this?" I ask as I look at her exquisite pearl ring.

Nancy giggles. "It's too late now. The state of Hawaii says we're married. Personally, I think this was the perfect Valentine's Day surprise."

"We've set the bar sky high. We're together because of your Christmas message and then we got married on Valentine's Day. What's next?"

"I don't know. Rogue keeps teasing me about Tristan's propensity to go to Paris on a random Tuesday. Until I met you, I never quite understood the appeal of his methods. Now that you've turned me into a free-spirited traveler, the idea has some merit."

"I can't argue with you there, Mrs. Hudson. But I think we'll have a few scores to settle with our family and friends first. I know Ketki was lobbying to be a full-scale bridesmaid in your wedding, instead of merely a flower girl. Lord knows what Jett and Diamond will say about the fact that we left them out of our celebration."

"Yeah, I know. I dread telling Savannah and Shelby. I don't want them to get the wrong idea. It wasn't because I didn't want them there. It felt special with only the two of us. It's as if we've shed the baggage of our pasts. As much as I love my kids, when I look at them, I see glimpses of George. I didn't want the ghost of him to interfere with our day."

"I understand. I think our friends will get it too. This was just a spur of the moment decision made out of pure love. We've made no secret of our love for each other or our plans for forever."

"That's true. I think the kids figured it out even before I did."

I raise my eyebrows as I smirk playfully at my wife. "But, you've got it all figured out now, don't you?" I ask, tongue-in-cheek. "You do love me?"

"More than I ever thought possible."

"Besides, it's not our fault Casey had exams and Ketki, Shelby, and Mark are at a gaming convention. When everybody's free, we'll just have a huge party back home and everyone can witness the power of a well-written Christmas message," I tease with a wink.

Nancy picks up a heavy lei from a nearby table and places it around my neck. "Thank you for helping me find the real woman who was buried under a lifetime of heartache and broken dreams. I am so grateful you believed in me. I love you, Rex Hudson. I'm honored to be your wife."

"I love you too, Mrs. Hudson. Boy, that has a nice ring to it, doesn't it?"

"It is simply the best," my wife says as we walk down the beach hand-in-hand with the sun setting behind us.

# Note from the Author

Dear Reader,


Thanks for giving my novella a read. If you liked reading about people who are not so stereotypical, then I've got good news…


… there's more.


Identity of the Heart is the first novel in the Hidden Hearts Series and it introduces the primary characters who work at Ink'd Deep.


Ivy wanted to shake up her life and come out of her shell a little.

But not like this.

Online dating was supposed to be fun — not change everything you thought you knew about yourself.

When Tristan is brought into solve a case of identity theft, he's sure he'll find a textbook case of cat fishing.

What he finds isn't like any textbook he's ever read.

The question is will anyone be happy he solved the mystery?

If you love sweet romance with a hint of mystery, Identity of the Heart is for you.

~Mary

Because love matters, differences don't.

# ACKNOWLEDGEMENTS

No book ever gets written in a vacuum. I often get story ideas from conversations I've overheard in the grocery store or in a restaurant. In this case, the tiny nugget of the storyline about how to find love the second time around came from the inspiring story of Toni, the epically cool mom of one of my high school buddies. Congratulations on your new marriage.

Sometimes when you write characters in a series, one of them seems to get orphaned in the middle of the book and you don't get to tell the rest of their story. Writing a novella was the perfect opportunity to tell you Nancy's story.

Thank you to Justin Crawford and Kathy Faltinson for your help with proofreading, Brianna Tubbs for editing, Kathern Watts and Becca Draper-Ristanovic for beta reading, and Lacey Redding for your expert help with promotion. I couldn't be the author I am without your help.

A huge shout-out to my fans who continue to show they believe that because love matters, differences don't.

# RESOURCES

**If you need help immediately, call 911.**


**National Domestic Violence Hotline:**

800-799-SAFE (7233) or 800-787-3224 (TDD)


**National Sexual Assault Hotline:**

1-800-656-HOPE (4673)


**Domestic Shelters.org**— A tool that enables you to find a domestic violence shelter in your area by ZIP Code or address. You can search by the specific service you need. There are also informative articles about how to help someone who may be a victim of domestic violence or sexual abuse.


**RAINN** (Rape, Abuse, Incest National Network) — The nation's largest anti-sexual assault organization. RAINN operates the National Sexual Assault Hotline at 1.800.656.HOPE and the National Sexual Assault Online Hotline at rainn.org, and publicizes the hotline's free, confidential services; educates the public about sexual assault; and leads national efforts to prevent sexual assault, improve services to victims and ensure that rapists are brought to justice.

**When Georgia Smiled**—A Foundation created by Robin McGraw to create and advance programs that help victims of domestic violence and sexual assault live healthy, safe and joy-filled lives. Initiatives include a phone app that helps create a safety plan for use in domestic violence date rape situations, education initiatives for use in high school and college settings and support programs for women.

# About the Author

I have been lucky enough to live my own version of a romance novel. I married the guy who kissed me at summer camp. He told me on the night we met that he was going to marry me and be the father of my children.

Eventually, I stopped giggling when he said it, and we've been married for more than thirty years. We have two children. The oldest is a Doctor of Osteopathy. He is across the United States completing his residency, but when he's done, he is going to come back to Oregon and practice Family Medicine. Our youngest son is now tackling high school and where he is an honor student. He is interested in becoming an EMT.

I write full time now. I have published more than thirty books and have several more underway. I volunteer my time to a variety of causes. I have worked as a Civil Rights Attorney and diversity advocate. I spent several years working for various social service agencies before becoming an attorney.

In my spare time, I love to cook, decorate cakes and of course, I obsessively, compulsively read.

I would be honored if you would take a few moments out of your busy day to check out my website,

MaryCrawfordAuthor.com. While you're there, you can sign up for my newsletter and get a free book. I will be announcing my upcoming books and giving sneak peeks as well as sponsoring giveaways and giving you information about other interesting events.

If you have questions or comments, please E-mail me at Mary@MaryCrawfordAuthor.com or find me on the following social networks:

Facebook: www.facebook.com/authormarycrawford

Website: MaryCrawfordAuthor.com

Twitter: www.twitter.com/MaryCrawfordAut